3'D' LOVE

DESIRE TO DEFINE OUR DESTINY

JEEVAN

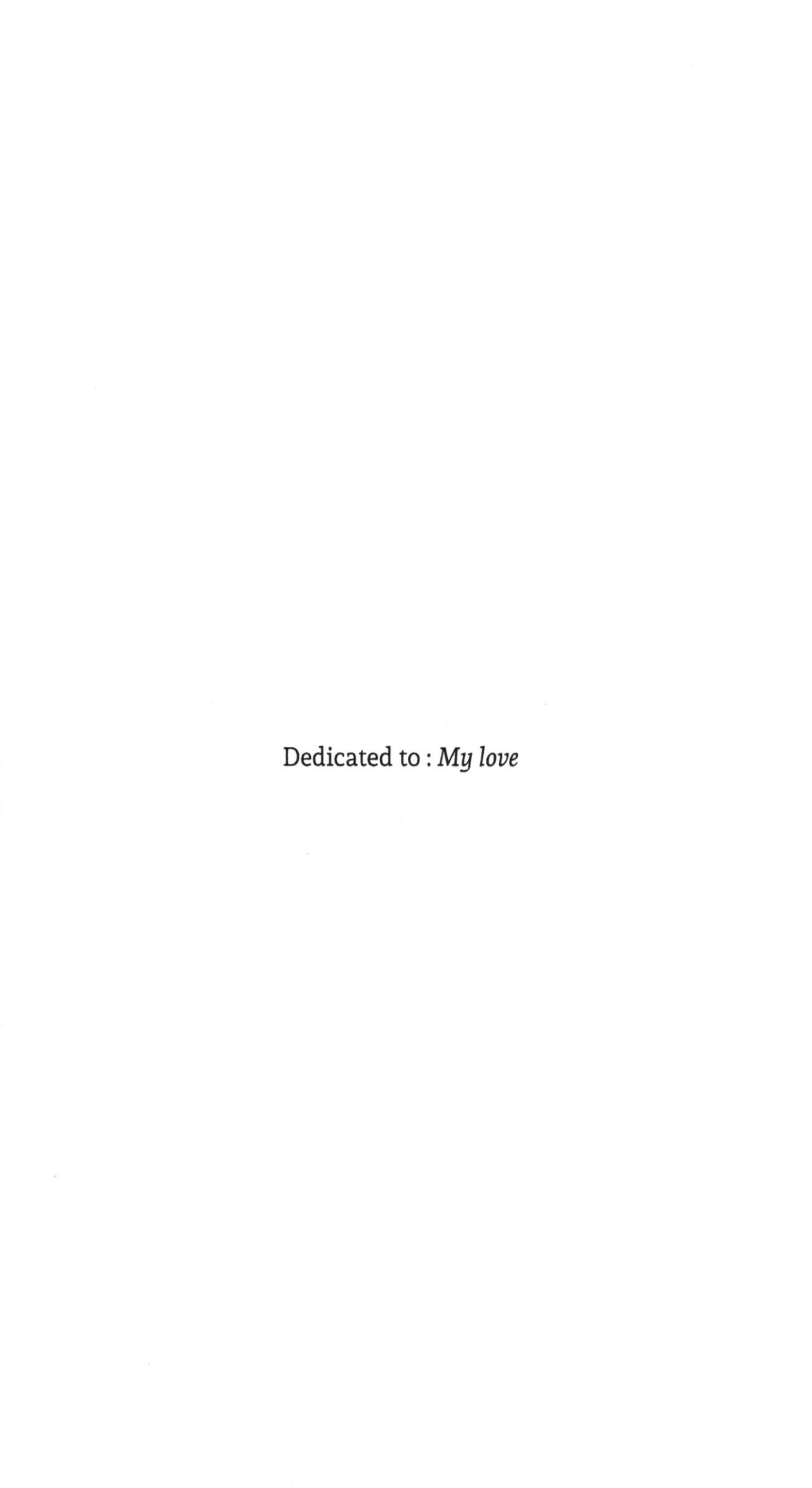

Dedicated to : *My love*

Contents

1

Chapter 1

"*Where did it start?*"

It was the 11th of September and the sun was about to group it-self, still I can feel it. I am about to let go of the lobby room. Woah wait I have not introduced where it started. A very good grouping networking sort of application called hago. By the time I started my journey with it there were few games where everyone could chill with one another, without having knowledge of each other. lol !

So I am about to let go of the lobby room and suddenly the brightest star "came into my living life" no no entered into the lobby room. A 20-year old babyish texted me with "HI'.We exchanged our names'She is PRACHI' and opening part's in a put feelings way and suddenly I asked for her number. lil being troubled lil poor usability lil got worked up and lil of a questioning mind.

What happened nearest? As had in mind she said no. I was put at a loss and angry too.We both are about to let go of. I do not have knowledge of what came up suddenly in her mind. She dropped her number. As expected, sudden things will also take place...lol...

This is how and this is where it started..

ϷϷϷ

12 of September 12th was the second day that I texted her for the first time that her things were not fixed with a warm good morning desire. There our journey started, officially day 1 and un-officially day 2 has gone through, we settled down in our positions and got time to have knowledge of each other's living.

So it has been 4 days since she came into my life. weeks passed and we are happy, laughing, foolish, what now! nothing! She said that she fell for someone.I smiled I am happy i am ready i am of a questioning mind and i am fucked.Everything is going well.

some-where I am over worked up cause my heart says i am that some-one she fell for. hmm gone red(blushed).

She started making moves in that some-one in every point of view gave the story to me and pointed to me.She said one day she is going to put forward, use him. I was making a mind-picture how I could put forward, into using myself to myself. foolish isn't it?

Finally the Day came she called me to the private lobby room again and my heart rate was quicker than lead fired from the gun train, my mini me and I were talking to each other and that's it.

It is not me seriously, it was some-one else, I am not that some-one she praised all the day. For the first time in our history that some-one came in between us and he is none other than her current lover (Prajwal).

As usual, I desire pleasure to be meeting you -pleased to be meeting you, Bye-Bye.

He looks like a thousand years old across from a monkey family, a small, long-eared horse-like animal, does not even have knowledge of our low level of development language, Not from our state, how they will keep in touch (with), Even his name sounds like buhahua. what makes her love him, what is he up to, what did he do that she was stamped with and talking like an old man in order of religion drunken monkey for all the day.

Why I am too had a part in her, Why i am having thoughts too far, cause i am in love with her. By day 4 I felt like she was the one for the rest of my life..So now all i can do is to act like there is nothing in my mind. I used to wait for her to profit from college every-day so that I could have a voice call, But now I am not interested anymore to give attention to her solid waste about him...

Days gone through, weeks passed! !Mr.prajwal is unhealthy for Prachi. I am not affected by this because I am in love with her, i have gone through their relationship, their love and their joining together, there is no love and there is no joining together.

She is in love with him only because she is 19 years old who seeks/influence for good-looking hanky panky world.It is so simple it is not love it is lust.Even though I said the same thing that he is unhealthy to her, she gets in a bad state of mind by my words.

I do not need to waste my time putting forward my feelings in the direction of her. It is right even if she kicks me out of her life or anything but i do not need him to be in her living cause he is not the one.

Again the day comes when I offer to her at last. As had in mind she said it is not good and that he is the only one that she is going to marry. I attempted my best to move my love to her again as I had in mind, not working those rules at all..

The most very sad thing here is that she still has not offered to him still. It doesn't suggest that the love only has existence only if the one in the grouped in 2 says they love you, But it means feeling, no one of them knows what exactly is that emotion.

"

What now!"

She used to use up 90% of her leisure time with me. We used to talk for hours and hours, we used to have amusement all the time.

What I am going to say is she has to do all these things with him. But why with me? Okie, let's take it to be true that I am given to her as bestie.But not fair/allowed to say, talk up with my bestie after 12AM without affecting my current lover.

Is that a secret love? acting falsely? get attraction to be made of 2 parts? OR nothing/something what? ?I have the responsibility for all these!!

She likes him and her mind-limited condition decides that this is called love. Even though she knows that he is not the one, she is making it seem, cause she doesn't need to get forced, put fear into any person not in the group. In Fact he is a secret lover.

NO the very thing FRIEND.Finally. she asked Mr.prajwal: Are you going to marry me? He said yes but only if my parents took you. So in his point of view their parents are not going to say yes to her anyway so he is not going to marry her. that's it. she just held for a few seconds and said parting words to him, he is positive to go back with the same.

No unreadiness at all. a little cold this is what people name a clear love..This is the end of the Mr.prajwal story now.

ᗡᗡᗡ

As I had in mind again now my line got clear but I am not the reason behind their breakup. lol not breakup just nonsense..So I kept in touch with her every-day to outline her attention. fixed regular order of acting days calls notes hago wide chitchats and so on and so on....

Till time-stamp it is me and her with few of the going past, through cloud friends at hago, before her i have few good/bad friends in hago.

Particularly 2 of them are pavani and pallavi from nearest and same district.pavani already offered me earlier literally she is with a diseased mind about me. We met twice in the real World and had a good time. There is nothing much to make, be moving in pavani or pallavi as they are not chief characters or roles in my life/story.

When prachi came into my living world everything changed, all my odd life was done. So pavani used to watch us being alone in private and personal broads, So that it makes her full of desire for what others have and angry in addition.

One all right night-fall pavani texted prachi with no news given to me. pavani over reacted on prachi and said that i am her current lover and we are going to marry soon.

Prachi sent me all the viewing output picture of their talk and pavani give order against like an american treasure to do not disclose this to me,
The most important thing is i do not even have knowledge of when i became pavani current lover with out my taking/initial-part. foolish persons in general. !

It just seriously made an angry protest to pavani for covering all over false rumores, But this is where i should appreciate her and say it is pleasing to her instead of the noises of a dog on her like a dog.

somewhere prachi felt so bad and unsafe, unsafe of what?

Still this makes everyone puzzle faces. Very next day I still have that evening thing... A new whatsapp note from prachi. I was not a stranger to that note but still i always have in mind some good from her, i opened it..! My eyes were filled with tears, My heart ran quicker than ever and my hand kept shaking with cold (fear) and i am without knowledge of what I should reply.

"

What is the note could be?"

ᗡᗡᗡ

The note from prachi is.. why don't we get married?

yeah all my religion-like requests, all my trials finally came true.This is all because of pavani false rumour, where prachi went into unsafe zone 5 that she is going to not see me.

Now what?What should I say? There is nothing to respond to , as I have already decided. Maybe to the World , prachi is merely one person, but to me, she is my entire world.

My inner voice has said that, However I asked her to give me some time as I have waited for ages for this and now I was asking for some time? why?
It's simple, there is something I want her to know about my past and present.

You read about an imaginary character who had a lot of middle grade fantasies and had a lovable nature up until this point.. AHAN!!! Now get ready to be surprised ...

As an introduction , I'm Pranav from a middle class family in the south of India.I,like everyone,lead a frightful,insidious life covered in a prestigious mask and utterly consumed by filthy desires. That is why I was married so early in my life.

Is that what you are saying now? (W.T.F)is that all?
Then you should wash your mouth.

Yes I love prachi, yes i am married, yes i have a daughter, yes i'm not employed, and yes,i do not belong to her caste.

In all seriousness, does it matter when someone truly falls in love with someone. Does it matter when someone truly falls in love with someone?

Let me put all your blank faces in suspense until we release the 1st section of the book. For now I'll continue forward...

Our two months together have flown by and we've been chatting for hours like there's no tomorrow. I don't even know how they passed. We've finally decided to meet in person.

The first time we met with zero expectations occurred on the 26th of October 2019 at around 8PM. We met unexpectedly. It isn't a date, it's just casual.

Therefore, I was instructed to exit at the specific halt called gajuwaka. She came with a chunny robe and track pants with a tee, and I wasn't expecting anything more than that but still she looks gorgeous.

As I mentioned, i just checked my height with her, haha... Lol, I haven't ever said hello to her in person, so yeah, we're about the same height, no big difference from what I expected.

"I stink," she says in the first word she says. Wait, what? How can she say that? Yea, I was totally drunk that day, but I didn't plan for her to point this out to me. It was strange, but even I enjoyed it. I threw a fake smile on the face of his younger brother as he walked along with her.
     A ten-minute walk and nonsync conversations later, we parted ways.

That's all for our first meeting. Nothing spectacular happened, no xoxo, but it was enjoyable nonetheless.
On my way back to my hometown, I again took the bus, and all night I smiled and blushed, and sleep soundly.

ϸϸϸ

Apparently everything is fine.She announces she is going on a vaccation, but she will go to ger grandmother's house alone.I take this a hint to ask me to go with her.

On the other hand , the grandmother's house is just 20 kilometers away from my neighbourhood.
So i prepared myself for our second meeting and waited with great expectations this time. She left her home at a certain time and shared me a llive location for easy tracking. with my curiosity, I tracked her through that live location.

Her jingle bells orange top and loose hair(wet) with a white bottom caught my attention from a mile away. She took a train and i too went inside.

She texted me!! Where are you? I just walked straight through the entire compartment to find her.
Ass she reserved a seat for me, i blushed again and again.

I sat quite opposite to her diagonally, on the phone with her. A bit shy, But why? we both were smiling.
After a while, the next seat became available, and i offered it to her.

While on the train we talked endlessly. so, I leaned in to kiss her hand and she reacted in a millisecond by taking it back. oh my god,what happend? I'm so ashamed!

Although i understand her feelings, since it was a train, how can she allow a boy to kiss her hand in front of public?. On the other hand, i believe i have a right to kiss her hand but not a french one.
Initially disappointed.

After reaching 80% of our destination, we hadd to get off and catch another train, which is when hher relatives appeared at ndd station. Once again i was completely clueles.

Finally we reach her cousin called Pooja who came to receive her, i gave them a proper farwell from there by giving books and t-shirt.

I planned to visit her a third time, I was pumped to see her again and i hopped on a bike to start my journey. Unfortunately, the bike gave me a trouble halfway. It took hours to get repaired it got stuck in the middle of the highway.

it is already 9:30 iin the evening, I wanted to see her at any cost, Buut this is not theright time for her. She is at her grandmother's house. I was upset and saw a bus crossing me which leads to her village. I ran after the bus in a cinematic fashion and i caught it.

As 10'O clock approached, shops were preparing to close. I grabbed soe sweets candy's from a sweet shop. i took an autorickshaw and went to her place. it's 10:30 now.

At this time, its really hard for her to make it to meet me. BUt she is really gutsy and brave to come out of her backyard and forge a path to meet me. We spoke for few seconds and she took what i got for her from the shops earlier. we are partways now..! she went back inside.

My insides are both happy and sad, why? a hug from her would have been nice.But she was not able to make it. I didn't return, i was waited outside blindly, we are keep on texting and requesting her to come out again.

Finally she came out, but she is very terrified of the timing and the place. there was no reason to forcefully hug her, but it did feel like a hug from each of us.

> "*it was quite an open place where i hugged her for the first time. So i took her in to the darkest place*

where we would not be seen by anyone. I embraced her and held her tightly for about five minutes. she wants to go back inside, i grabbed her hand and pulled her towards me and hugged her again."

"*We are in a pin drop silence where we can hear the sound of our hearts beating. I can hear her breathing, so mind says to kiss her. I kissd her lips and tried to eat them, i was gently licking her lips and toungue and trying to get to her soul.*"

"*Her hands stopped me from touching her insecure areas, so i wispered in her ear that it's ok, So then i reached inside her top and it was very hot though and both her boobies are really deicious and stunning to hide in love.*

I'm very pleased with her waist ,her lips, her neck, her boobs, her hands, and her shoulders, Everything tastes like heaven to me."

The late night ended up so romantically, we don't even know how it happened. it was 3 AM in the morning, we had spent 4 hours on xoxo. i couldn't believe it. she told me now it was time to leave. I hugged onemore time and i headed back to my hometown. it was a long walk from there to the first bus, since there was no transport facility at the time.

The following day, we were flooded with the incredible memories of last night. we plan to return for 4th time again at the same time with the same expectations as yesterday.

Asusual i went, she came, I was given a bounty with love, so we hugged for about 2 minutes, not knowing what was happening whe the lights turned on by their elders and they started searching for her like never before. I thought we got caught by their grand parents, and i was bit scared.

In a split second we knew today is not or day, and i left the place and walked all the way to the bus terminal and waited there till the morning for the first bus to come again. very next day that she packed up her self to head back to her hometown, i accompany her, this time her cousins and grandparents are with her too. we had a great time in return.

the memories of the past few days were unforgettable and cherished.

ᗐᗐᗐ

In an instant, she completely stopped texting me and her phone went off. i was deeply upset what happend.suddenly a pop appears from her reminding me that i am supposed to wait for her positive sign before i text or call her. i am going to reply her but it was too late she turned off her phone again.

"what happend?"

"

finally i got a message that everything collapsed."

what happend i asked, my parents came to know that we met that night she responded.

After constantly asking how and when this was happened?

She responded with, 'My parents are most important to me when it comes to priorities':'Sorry i cannot make it any longer.I just promised them i would never speak to you again.'

"those words broke my heart and caused me to burst into tears"

My fault i should not supposed to force her to come back at that night, i just fucked my own happiness and even i dragged her and thrown in this shit.

I suffered, I cried, I yelled, was there anything else i could do?
After a while though, she texted me again apologizing. There were tears wiped away automatically and my heart started singing 'Everynight in my dreams' at that message .

Then she started explaing things what happend to her.

Her mother inquired about the 4 hour night spent together, but somehow mother was not sure about inch to inch. still, girl was stunned and unable to comprehend, A bunch of questions hits her in a trance,

"what? why? How? When?"

Despite finally opening up, the girls mother suddenly slapped her and then began asking her tons of questions.May be every well being mother from a tradational big family would do the same.

Her mother finally agreed for her to explain. She just emphatically stated that the man who came to her that night is just a friend of mine.He was just passing through and wanted to hand me few sweets to our family.Besides that nothing happend, she said

Mom : why at night? Why not during a day?

girl : he did not make time for me to meet, he was just passing through!!

Mom : what you did is unacceptable and we should talk to your father who is really upset!!

girl heart flutters at multiple speeds and she has no clue what to say and how to handle her father!!!
This is it happend still i have no clue of how this got exposed to her mother?

then she said that someone from the neighbourhood wandered up to us and reported the next day to my grandmother.My granny told my parents everything that happened that night,But no one is unsure in a clear way. Luckily i managed to get them to understand in a crystal clear way.
Her father called me one day without any prompting and warning sign. I picked up and and i was very polite, he later told me that he called me to warn me about her daughter and her family.
i apologized and kept quiet. that the way it ended up for me with her father(my future in law).
The situation has changed now, Her parents have started taking her mobile phone after 8PM everyday.While we have been struggling, But we are still together.
We use to talk as often as we could during her study hours. she became everything to me, She is the only one who can make me feel happy and sad.

ϷϷϷ

JEEVAN

ᔆᔆᔆ

ᔆᔆᔆ

2
Chapter 2

There aren't many friends in her life. In other words, she's inward but also outgoing. she use to say how much she admires each of her friends and how great they are, also male besties play an important role in girl's lives. No surprise here.

Then one fine afternoon, unbeknownst to me,i really wanted o talk to her.she had finished her classes, so i called she did not pick up,and i called ten times in a row in the hopes she would pick it up. she called me back and i became furious and shouted at her. she said she went out with her friend to collect the delivery.

i asked what in the world is so important than me. who is she you went with atleast you would have informed me i said.

it's him my friend pullarao and i went to collect his delivery.
it was then i became more angry and hung up the phone call. I was then left with a negative shade of that pullarao in my mind.

Everytime she mention his name my blood boil fasten than the sun.i was pretending each day that he is so cute and calm, but in my innermost thoughts,i felt like the most ugliest bugs are crawling on my body.

This time no full stop for disappointment.

ᐯᐯᐯ

Having been through all these bad situations, we decided to meet in person again. This time I traveled alone to see her at 5 in the morning.

I took the train to the station and then public transport to get to the bus stop where her father dropped her off. We took the bus and it was a 90-minute journey. Today's plans are in motion.

She went inside the collage and promised I that she would come back within 15-20 minutes after filling out an application.

Since the gate keeper refused to let me inside with her, I waited outside at the nearby pan shop for about 10-15 minutes.

Although it's ok, she needs to let me know well in advance so I can set my self up for 2 hours instead of just waiting blindly.

It was too hot and 40 degrees centigrade outside but atleast she came and I am content. We are now waiting for the bus to cityside and I asked her where would you like to have lunch, she said no, she is heading back home.

Her rejection for lunch has never been explained to me, she has never explained why she has made her decisions.

The only thing I know is that I became comical by waiting and dreaming for things that will never happen we took the bus again and i was asking her in front of the public and she was rude. She wore a lemon yellow dress that day.

After we arrived at her stop, and still I asked her for a reason, she didn't even bother to answer. I dropped her off, and I was looking for a bus to go home, so for this impression I have to ask myself, did I really deserve to be treated like this after travelling 800 kilometers for her?

i'am angry, being angry or upset with your loved ones is a common phenomenon. But when the anger stems from betrayal or disappointment then the sadness and hurt is the underlying emotion of your anger

Her apology came back after a few days, but this time I didn't want a fucking apology. I needed a reason, so she explained she was afraid of meeting me out in public for fear of getting into trouble again.

Who in the world is watching us in particular, her thinking was not in a correct path. Perhaps, she is insecure of something that something is me.

The most exasperating thing is no one watch when she visits restaurants with pullarao, no insecurities while she takes a seat backside of him on the bike.

she is okay with sharing lunch boxes with pullarao but not a single joyride with me.

Then I need to ask her where I stand in her life and what my priorities are, but thinking this way makes me feel bad and makes her perceive me as less important than pullarao, so I need to settle this issue before I go any farther.

ᏮᏮᏮ

Security is increasingly important in a relationship; if i'am second-guessing my relationship because a guy shows up, you need to reevaluate your stance.

My relationship should be my first preference here in my

view.

I do not need to have a fight with pullarao just to justify my unfounded, speculative notions and i'm her first priority, all i can say loud is i don't like pullarao simple.

My conversations with her were full of things I asked her and things I expressed we argued and we cried. Afterwards, she said that I'd get no more problems and so she promised me that none of these things will ever happen again.

> *"If you feel attacked or vulnerable by your*
> *girlfriend's friend, communicate it to her.*
> *She isn't a mind-reader, she can't know what's*
> *going inside your head.*
>
> *Don't go chasing after the idea of them together, it*
> *will only bring heartbreak for you.*
> *Tell you girlfriend about what bothers you about*
> *him and what you would like to do about it.*
> *Tell her why you don't like her hanging out with*
> *him.*
> *Try to figure out why it bothers you so much.*
> *Tell her it that you aren't comfortable with him*
> *hanging around you guys all the time.*
> *Thats all i have done actually everything sorted*
> *out."*
>
> *"Our relationship is too strong mentally now we*
> *need to talk about how to interact physically, so we*
> *both agreed to hook up, so we reached Kommadhi*
> *for the first time, and first time for her to be with a*
> *boy in a hotel room, but not for me (don't think*

*dirty) these things don't mean anything but it's
awkward to find out where to start and where to*
"
stop. **"**

asuaual i started with a beautiful hug, but a beautiful hug
will never turns on anyone.Also i don't want to talk dirty to
turn her on,It's really important her to know
i like kissing her i focus always what excatly she likes. i just
steer clear of "i'am a good kisser": It can unwittingly make
her think of the other lips you've encountered.

Sex is one of the most powerful gifts God ever created.
It was designed to bring a man and woman together in a
physical, emotional and spiritual bond that would create,
pleasure, intimacy and also procreation.

Men and women approach sex very differently. Men
make love to feel loved. Women need to feel loved to make
love.

We started fooling around, lying on the bed, which was
really comfortable. When we tried to dissolve two different
in the name of love, we are really nervous because it was
her first time having penetrative sex, and her body showed
it, so of course I turned to liquid courage.

We get going and her mind was saying, 'Yes, she want
this,' but her pain was 'rejecting' me. We tried various
positions for access and comfort,

Just like how you worry about your own endowment,
she's concerned about what you'll think of her private
parts,So when you go down on her using oral i feeded her
vagina some compliments.

Moan it up. As much as you like to make her scream, she
likes to hear me to get into it, too and it was fun until i got
up to get me a hot towel and i saw the blood on the bed.

Even my dirty mind says that i wish i could had a blowjob but she seems like she is not that seasoned in that department.

Having cuddled, loved, hugged, kissed, and shared sex, I think this is a sign of marriage in the spiritual realm, yes we are married in the spiritual realm because of our love.

The three days we spend together in the same room mean that she comes to me under the pretext of collage. We stay together until evening and she pretends her parents to be coming directly from collage.

I dropped her off at her stop on new year's eve, and her father picked her up that evening, so we are having fun together as usual.

ᛏᛏᛏ

"Happy new year by the way...!!!

ᛏᛏᛏ

"

the day comes finally. i just texted her to know where she was?
At home she said.

i was waiting at the street end and asked her to come out for an hour.

she refused but somehow managed to come.

Unlike that time, I was in a car where a black mercedes followed by three cars and I invited her inside so she could have a seat. We went towards a huge mall with a red carpet and all the staff and crowd welcomed us in as we walked there.

She just remained calm since she couldn't believe it had just happened. I took her inside the mall and when we passed through the door we were greeted with lakhs of rose petals as well as thousands of balloons and colored flakes.

She was speechless and, for the first time, asked me what all this means in the middle of the mall where there was a rotating wheel that was already decked out for us.

As she presented me with a platinum ring set, I gave her a sign not to speak and to watch the crowd cheering for us. I just showed her my hand and she complied with my request.

It's been 30 seconds since I proposed, and they were all still saying aww and aww. I just kneeled down and went slowly and the crowd went slowly as well. You would have thought it wouldn't take her long to say yes.

Once again I glanced at my right hand side, and there were her parents smiling and she was even further shocked. They gave her a solid yes and she put a ring on it, and that's it, we're engaged!

When I stepped forward to kiss her, I was a bit shy. I closed my eyes and was about to kiss her, but a huge noise blew suddenly and someone behind me kept disturbing me.

I opened my eyes and he was a conductor, the sound was a bus horn, and I was in the bus traveling to my hometown after having dropped her off at her stop on new year's eve; I was in a dream.

"This was a very bright and fruitful start to the new year that day because it was a beautifully cinematic dream again.

ÞÞÞ

"

Due to her busyness with her projects and collage, we had a bit of an argument as usual, our fight usually ends in us becoming enemies.

This time was bit acrimonious after completing our argument, she should call me to resolve or she should keep calm, but what actually happened is different.

He was the next caller and she had promised me that she would never hurt me in his topic, but she did the same again.

Why doesn't she call me instead of arguing and talk about everything?

She remains unconcerned about my call even though it is on hold; is she really thinking that giving him my time is filthy behavior? What should I do now?

This time when I finally got a response, I just asked for one thing from her. I asked her to call my boyfriend and set up a conference call. She declined.

I became mad and psycho and kept asking again and again. I really wanted to confront this monster.

In the end, she saved him even though I begged her to do so, she doesn't want him to get hurt by me but she is okay if I get hurt by him this time!

This is what always disappoints me in her, and this time was no exception to her always letting me down! This situation was not hurting me, but it was breaking my heart!

I said to her to either remove Pullarao from your life or remove me. I have already gone through three stages in my relationship. Will my fiance choose me over someone else? Is that what you call love?

As long as she acted in her own best interest put an end to pullarao and i'm now happy.

I'm a person who will not tolerate the word 'no' as long as they follow my lead - even if they are uneasy or uncomfortable for me they must say yes. If she says yes, I will say yer, if she says no, then I will make sure to change it to yes.

It seems like we usually argue over every tiny point like I mentioned earlier. I hope this is what love is all about. I need respect, respect, and infinite love I am not getting that right now.

I think husbands or wives have rights over others. If everyone disagrees with me it doesn't make any sense.

Although there have been many arguments, miscommunications, and misundertandings, one thing is certain: all of these disturbances had never dominated our love because we are no longer in love, it is always with us. It has been almost three years since we first got together.

The godessess in this country are like 108, but if there is really one then I will call her my godesses because she always protects me, always stands for me, even if she is rude at times if anyone asks me what is special about her I cannot answer, because one thing is clear, without her nothing would be special in my life.

The girl is done with her studies and she just got placed at one of the best multinational companies in the world with a great package, and I was struggling to get a job, but she is still ready to marry me even though I am unemployed her thoughts and her nature make me fall in love with her right away.

I'm not even eligible to ask her father for a marriage because I'm unemployed, not a tall man, and I have no income to support my family. The most important thing is that I do not belong to her religion or caste, no father would accept someone with those qualities.

Usually, I tried my best to ask them as expected, but they didn't accept anyway, even her parents fixed the marriage without her knowledge. I was shocked because she agreed to them. I was literally sobbing on the road like I lost everything.

ᗰᗰᗰ

Afterwards, I was told by her friend that she accepted the marriage on purpose, yes it is a strategy, once again I took her for granted, but now things are back on track again the strategy is if she rejects the marriage, they will stop her from working and enslave her, they will do house arrest.

She accepted on purpose because she thought we could find a way to get rid of everyone who was negative about me. During all this time her friends and colleagues were suggesting I was unfit for her life, but she still found a way to win. One day she called me and said to meet her at the spot where we first met by 8AM the following day.

After I rushed and took a bus by night, I arrived at the place by 4AM. After waiting for four hours, she finally arrived with a luggage, accompanied by her father, who dropped her off at the stop.

The way she walked in the bus this time and sat behind me even though she is acting as if she is talking to a stranger reminds me of our old days when we used to travel.

Her hands and finger are covered in mehendi, she has a diamond ring on her finger, and her bridal makeup is still on her face. She smells different this time from when we used to travel.

After listening to what she said she became engaged with a branch manager at Amex and earns up to 50L/PA so, after a few moments, my smile faded. I asked her to stop.

If this is what you wanted to say then please don't say anything. If that's the case then I'd like to step out of the bus i said.

Although she is not all done, i don't want to listen anything negative because I am too exhausted to process such things, so at the bus depot we board another bus which had already been reserved for us by her. Once we boarded, we settled down and cried for a bit.

Despite her calm nature, i poked her and she said not to bother her we both slept in different directions we both arrived in Bangalore by 11AM, and she had booked a cab with me.

We got to the enclave using an elevator and were escorted to the first floor where a room number 1001 was located she handed me the keys to the apartment.

When I opened the door, it was a new apartment filled with the furniture we needed and the watchman came to me and said, "Sir, here is your flat name board, good luck", whereupon I was stunned to see:

>>>???∈ ??<<<

♡ Pʀ?ɴ?? & Pʀ??ʜ I ♡

???? ???????? & ??????? ???? ?????

♡♡♡

I was not in the mood to kiss her, but my eyes are still question marks. She took me to the restroom and asked me to take the ring off her finger, which I did.

She had told me to flush it, so I did.

It was the tightest hug ever as she said I could never be the kind of person to fuck someone and then marry another, and it was also on that day that I gave my everything to you at kommadhi that you became my husband, as well as this is our apartment we intend to live in as husband and wife.

From day 1 to engagement day she planned everything. From purchasing a condo to booking a marriage slot at the registry office i felt like I had won this world.

I kissed her to show my happiness and were sat on the sofa and she explained everything that happened in these days.

It's been months since we have laughed like this we spoke four hours nonstop and then we had some food and took a nap. I have four days before the wedding, so I left her in the apartment.

The next day, I went to my hometown to get all of my clothes and everything before going back to her

I kissed her again and this time she gave me a surprise by bringing my mother to witness us officially married. She is very brave.

No matter what she does in life, she will never make me doubt her commitment to me.

Those who claim women are weak should take a look at her,
Look at how strong and brave she is, how eminent she is, how magnificent she is, how just ultimate she is,

It is hard to describe her as she is the only one who can make

*me happy or sad, she is the only one i'll ever put my faith in i
promise to never let her down in my life,that is an oath...*

The honeymoon is a solemn important thing a symbol And it ought to be done well. I don't want an expensive honeymoon because I'm extravagant, but because a honeymoon is important and should be done properly.

We are sitting on our honeymoon bed in the honeymoon suite. We are in a state of honeymoon, in our honey month. These words are so sweet: honey, moon.

This bed is so big, we could live on it. We have been happily marooned, honey marooned, on this bed for days.

I actually had another surprise in store for me. She had fought with her parents for all these days and she finally convinced them to accept me as her son-in-law. Now my family is all happy.

*"That's it for Prachi and Pranav, their simple love
story with a happy ending "*

*"**THE END**
Thank you!!!"*

www.ingramcontent.com/pod-product-compliance
Lightning Source LLC
Chambersburg PA
CBHW020853160726
47993CB00004B/1632